A JIGSAW JONES MYSTERY

Super Special #4

The Case of the Santa Claus Mystery

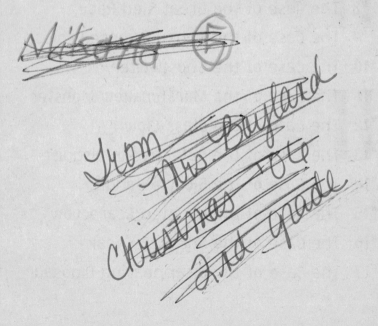

Nitscha

From Mrs. Baylord

Christmas '06

2nd grade

Read all the Jigsaw Jones Mysteries

And Don't Miss . . .

JIGSAW JONES SUPER SPECIAL #1
The Case of the Buried Treasure

JIGSAW JONES SUPER SPECIAL #2
The Case of the Million-Dollar Mystery

JIGSAW JONES SUPER SPECIAL #3
The Case of the Missing Falcon

JIGSAW JONES' DETECTIVE TIPS

Super Special #4

The Case of
the
Santa Claus Mystery

by James Preller
illustrated by Jamie Smith
cover illustration by R. W. Alley

A
LITTLE APPLE
PAPERBACK

SCHOLASTIC INC.
New York Toronto London Auckland Sydney
Mexico City New Delhi Hong Kong Buenos Aires

ISBN 0-439-79396-3

A condensed version of this story, "Jigsaw Jones: The Case of the Santa Claus Mystery," was published in *Very Merry Christmas Tales* in 2004.

12 11 10 9 8 7 6 5 4 3 2 1   6 7 8 9 10 11/0

Printed in the U.S.A.
First printing, October 2006

This book is dedicated to my editor, Shannon Penney, who rocks.

The author also acknowledges the charitable work performed by the staff and volunteers at Equinox, a nonprofit community agency that serves the Capital District area of New York.

— J.P.

CONTENTS

Chapter One
Bah Humbug!

Christmas was more than a week away, but I had heard the song "Rudolph, the Red-Nosed Reindeer" about five hundred times already. If you ask me, that's 487 times too many.

It's a big problem with Christmas, when you think about it. The songs are great, but they get crammed into a three-week period, like too many crayons in a box. I figure they need to spread them out over the year. Maybe hearing "Frosty the Snowman" in July would be kind of cool.

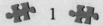

Or not.

Back to "Rudolph." The tune was good, but the words bugged me. Mostly, the other reindeer sounded cruel. Rudolph was different. He had a weird nose. So what? Did all the reindeer have to call him names? They couldn't let him play *any* reindeer games? What happened to the Christmas spirit?

Then Rudolph saved the day, and

everybody turned nice. They all wanted to be friends with the big hero. Yeesh. I hope Rudolph didn't fall for that. Where were they when Rudolph needed a real friend? Playing reindeer games, that's where!

I'm just saying, I'm a little disappointed in Comet and Dasher, Donder and Blitzen, and those other guys. Because a true friend is there through thick and thin, not just when Santa is giving you a big hug and telling everybody that maybe your nose isn't so bad after all.

But this Christmas, I had bigger problems to think about. My dad was turning into Scrooge. He said he wanted to cancel Christmas!

It all started at the dinner table on Friday night. It was the usual dinner with the Jones family — crowded. There were shouts, elbows, spilled milk, reaching, grabbing, pushing, shoving. And that was just Grams!

Only kidding. But dinner at our house is like a hockey game. I kept expecting my mother to blow a whistle and give my brothers two minutes each for roughing.

Daniel and Nicholas were arguing about PlayStation games. Hillary was saying she just wanted money for Christmas. Billy kept talking about a car he wanted. Rags sniffed around under the table, searching for scraps. And Mom was complaining about how she had to go to the mall . . . and how my dad still had to put up the lights outside . . . and how maybe we should get a fake tree this year because it was easier . . . and how everything cost so much money nowadays. . . .

That's when my father stood up. "I can't take it anymore," he announced. "I used to love Christmas. Now all anyone thinks about are presents and money!"

"Yeah, so?" Hillary asked.

My father frowned. "If it were up to me,

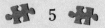 5

I'd cancel Christmas!" He carried his plate to the counter. "Excuse me," he said. "I think I'm going to step outside for a minute."

After he left, we sat in stunned silence for a few seconds. Then Billy asked, "Can I eat Dad's dessert?"

Chapter Two

Family Time

We didn't realize that my dad had left in the car ... until he pulled back into the driveway.

He walked into the house dragging a Christmas tree. A real one!

"Honey, what is this all about?" my mother asked.

"I'm sorry," he said. "I didn't mean to rant and rave like a crazy person."

"Yeah, that's our department," Billy joked.

My father laughed. "It just feels like we've lost our way a little bit," he said. "Christmas

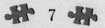

has become so stressful. People rushing around, honking horns, waiting in lines, spending money they don't even have."

I spoke up. "In school, I learned that Geetha Nair's family is from India. They celebrate *Diwali*. We could try that holiday instead," I suggested. "It's called the Festival of Lights, but it sounds like it's mostly about cleaning."

"Jigsaw!" Hillary scoffed. "That's ridiculous."

"The Jordans celebrate Kwanzaa," Nick said. "It sounds pretty good to me."

"My friend Isabelle says that her family is half-Christmas, half-Jewish," Daniel said,

 8

grinning. "We could try Hanukkah, I guess. It has eight days — a present for every day!"

"No, that's not the point," my father said. "There's nothing wrong with Christmas itself. We're just not celebrating it the right way. We've all gotten too materialistic."

"What does that mean?" I asked.

"It's become too much about things, and not enough about family," my father said. "That's why I got this tree. We're all going to decorate it together, and we're going to have fun!"

"But I have plans. . . ." Hillary protested.

"You heard your father, Hillary," my mother said. "We're going to do something nice together — or else!"

For a while there, I worried that "or else" was going to win. But once we got started, we had fun. Even Hillary. Grams baked sugar cookies. Billy brought down his guitar and played rockin' versions of Christmas tunes.

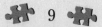

Then my mom pulled out the DVD of *A Charlie Brown Christmas*.

"Ah, a classic," my father beamed. "My favorite Christmas show ever."

After we watched that, we started talking about all of our favorite Christmas shows.

"Let's make a list," my father suggested.

"Oh, your father and his lists!" my mother groaned, laughing.

"Hey!" he protested. "I love lists!"

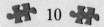

"So let's do it!" I cried.

We got to work on a list of the Ten Best Christmas Shows in the History of the World. Then we promised to watch every single one this year. Here's our list:

A Charlie Brown Christmas
How the Grinch Stole Christmas
A Christmas Story
The Polar Express

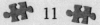

The Santa Clause
Elf
Rudolph, the Red-Nosed Reindeer
Miracle on 34th Street
Home Alone
A Christmas Carol

"Pretty good," Grams said, looking over the list when we finished. "But you have to add *It's a Wonderful Life*."

That's when I got a phone call from Sally Ann Simms. It sounded important. "I have a case for you," she said. "Are you still doing detective work over Christmas?"

"You bet," I replied. "A good detective is always on the job. For a dollar a day, I make problems go away."

We arranged to meet the next day. I hung up the phone and rushed back to the discussion. "You can't scratch *Elf* off the list," I cried. "He pours maple syrup on his spaghetti!"

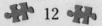

Chapter Three
His Busy Time of Year

Sally Ann Simms was only four years old. She weighed maybe thirty pounds — if her socks were filled with rocks. Which, come to think of it, was likely. Sally Ann liked rocks. She was that kind of gal.

The throwing-rocks kind.

Sally Ann Simms was one tough cookie. And in my line of work, I've met a lot of cookies. You see, I'm a detective. Jigsaw Jones, private eye. I have a partner named Mila Yeh. Together we've tackled ghosts, found missing paintings, and tracked down

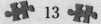
13

stolen bicycles. We've done it all, except for making it past the second grade.

Sally Ann came over on Saturday afternoon. Rags greeted her at the door, jumping and barking and licking, like it was the most exciting thing that had ever happened in his entire life. Rags did this every time somebody came to the door. Go figure. Still, Sally Ann made a big fuss over

him, petting him and wrestling and basically making him go bananas.

"You really love dogs, don't you?" I asked.

Sally Ann's eyes shone with joy. "Oh, yes," she squealed. "I'm crazy about dogs!"

I led Sally Ann into my basement office. I sat at my desk, and Sally Ann sat across from me. Rags waited upstairs (he hated two things in the entire world: the basement and stewed cabbage). Sally Ann's mood turned serious. She stared hard into my eyes. Her arms were crossed. "I want to meet Santa," she demanded.

I cracked open my detective journal. "Santa?" I repeated, scribbling down the name. "Last name?"

"Claus," Sally Ann said.

"Santa . . . Claus," I wrote.

"That's the one," Sally Ann said.

"Big white beard? Wears black boots and a red suit? Last seen driving a sleigh led by, let's see . . ." I flipped through the pages of

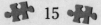

my journal and pretended to read, ". . . eight flying reindeer?"

Sally Ann didn't like being teased. She never cracked a smile. Instead, she rummaged inside her pink plastic pocketbook. She pulled out the head of a Barbie doll — that's it, just the head. Sally Ann frowned and continued poking around. She pulled out some baseball cards, a tissue (used, I suspect), a handful of rocks, beads, a hammer (!), and other assorted junk.

"Here," she finally said.

Sally Ann smoothed out a dollar bill on my desk.

She was serious.

Sally Ann Simms wanted to meet Santa Claus.

And it didn't seem like she would take no for an answer.

I asked her why.

She shrugged. "We have business to discuss," she mumbled.

I thought about Christmas. I still needed to get a present for Grams. It wasn't going to be much. Probably just a jar of skin cream. I only had thirty-seven cents to my name. I didn't think they sold jars that small.

And there sat good old George Washington. The first president of the United States. The father of our country. I cannot tell a lie: I stuffed old George into my pocket.

"It's a deal," I told Sally Ann. "But no promises. Santa is an important guy — and this is his busy time of year."

Chapter Four

The Secret Message

I woke up thinking about the case. I had already taken Sally Ann's money. Now I wasn't so sure it was a great idea. Money makes you do funny things.

My alarm clock read 7:23, Sunday morning. Rags lay in bed beside me. For a dog, he was a bed hog. I didn't mind, except when he breathed on my neck. Warm dog breath is gross. I think everybody can agree about that.

Even worse, Rags snored. For real. But other than that, I liked the big lug. He liked

me, too. A guy can tell. We were buddies. Rags stuck to me like chewing gum to the bottom of a gym sneaker.

It was Sunday. That meant no school. I still had plenty of work to do. Detectives don't rest until the case is solved. Unless, of course, we get really sleepy. Then we catch some shut-eye. But we always wake up and get right back to work.

I had to talk to Mila. In the detective

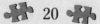

business, you can't be too careful. Spies are everywhere. That's why we sent each other messages in secret code. Plus, it was fun.

There was one little problem. Mila could crack any code in the book. That was her great talent. But I was dying to stump her. Just once, I wanted to come up with a code that even Mila couldn't figure out.

So I thought, and I thought, and I drank some grape juice, and I thought some more. Then it hit me like a ton of tinsel. (That's two thousand pounds of tinsel, folks.) The code was so simple, even a baby could figure it out. That's what I was counting on. Because sometimes the best place to hide something is out in the open. No one thinks to look there.

I cut a thin strip of white paper. I neatly wrote the message:

3SVƆ M3N V 3ΛVH 3M
V71W 0773H

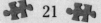 21

Rags watched while I worked. He was part Newfoundland, with lots of fur. Rags actually *liked* December's deep freeze, so he was the perfect messenger. I taped the note to the inside of his collar and opened the front door. A cold wind slapped my face.

"Go, boy," I ordered. "Go find Mila!"

Rags looked at me as if I were speaking a different language. And, come to think of it, I guess I was. But anyway . . .

I pointed down the block toward Mila's house. "Go on, Ragsy!"

Rags tilted his head and drooled.

"Deliver the message!" I commanded. Then I weakly added, "Arf, arf."

Rags curled up on the rug and shut his eyes.

Yeesh.

So I pulled on a sweater, my winter coat, hat, scarf, and gloves. I took the message from Rags' collar and trudged down the block to Mila's house.

Mila was out in her front yard. Get this, she was sitting on a sled. That was strange. Especially because there wasn't any snow on the ground.

She was singing. And like always, Mila made up her own words. The song was "Holly Jolly Christmas" — but not the way Mila sang it:

"Build a roly-poly snowman,
It's the best time of the year!"

"What are you doing?" I asked her.

"Positive thinking!" Mila answered cheerfully.

"Huh?"

"I want it to snow, Jigsaw. I want the

clouds to open up and drop a gazillion fluffy white snowflakes," Mila said happily. "I want to build snowmen and race in Lincoln Park with my sled. . . ."

"I don't know, Mila," I replied, glancing up at the clear sky. "Snow would be nice, but it doesn't look likely."

"It's not Christmas without snow," Mila protested.

I shrugged. "It's not Halloween, either." I handed her the note.

Mila stared at it for a long minute. She frowned. Mila looked baffled, bamboozled, befuddled, and bewildered.

Just my lucky day, I guess.

Chapter Five
Tracking Santa

Mila's stepmother, Alice, made big mugs of hot chocolate for us.

"Would you like a marshmallow with that, Jigsaw?" she asked.

I narrowed my eyes. "Is that a trick question?"

"No," Alice said, smiling.

"Then yes, thank you." I nodded. "A marshmallow would be nice."

Alice looked at Mila. "How about you, sweetie?"

Mila grunted, gnashing her teeth. Scraps

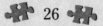

of paper were scattered across the table. Mila scribbled furiously.

"She's trying to crack a code," I told Alice.

Alice nodded. She quietly set a mug of hot chocolate in front of Mila, plopped a marshmallow on top, then left the room.

"Any luck yet?" I prodded Mila.

Mila leaned back in her chair. "I've tried every code I know," she confessed. "I've tried the alternate letter code, checkerboard code, substitution code, space code, telephone code — but nothing works!"

She was getting frustrated.

"It's a real brain-buster," I murmured with secret glee. "Do you give up?"

"Never," Mila replied.

Well, never is a long time. Two minutes later, Mila was asking for a hint.

I gave her a big one.

"You're not holding the paper the right way!"

Mila's eyes widened in shock. She turned the page upside down and read it out loud: "HELLO MILA! WE HAVE A NEW CASE."

"Gotcha!" I said.

"I thought my head was going to explode," Mila admitted, smiling.

Then I told her about my visit with Sally Ann Simms.

"Wow, I don't know, Jigsaw," Mila said doubtfully. "Santa Claus? That's big. I don't think we should mess around with Santa."

"I already took her money," I said. "You and I will split it, fifty-fifty."

"We can give it back," Mila suggested.

I shrugged. "You know me, Mila. Once I start a job, I have to finish it. Besides, think about it. Santa Claus. That's like the biggest mystery of all."

"So do you have any bright ideas?" Mila asked.

"I offered to bring Sally Ann to the mall," I

said. "They have a Santa in the department store."

Mila made a face. "How did that go over?"

"Like a lead doughnut," I answered. "Sally Ann said she wants to meet the real deal, not a phony toy-store Santa."

"Smart girl," Mila said. Her eyes suddenly twinkled with life. "I've got it! The Santa Tracker!"

"The Santa . . . what?"

"It's a Web site," Mila explained.

I stared at her with a blank expression.

"Haven't you heard of it, Jigsaw?" Mila said. "It tracks Santa on Christmas Eve, like a giant radar map."

"Great," I said. "Let's check it out."

We found Mila's father shopping on the Internet. Christmas music played from the speakers. You guessed it — it was "Rudolph, the Red-Nosed Reindeer."

"That's five hundred and one times," I noted.

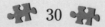 30

Mila turned to me. "What?"

"Never mind."

Mr. Yeh typed in the address for the Web site. It was cool but disappointing. Mila read the home page out loud: *"We track Santa for you every Christmas Eve, following his progress as he delivers gifts around the world."*

Mr. Yeh pointed out that the site had lots

of interesting stuff on it. There were recipes, games, the history of Santa, and more.

"Games are fun," I told Mr. Yeh. "But this is business."

Mr. Yeh's eyebrows arched toward the ceiling. "Business, eh? Don't tell me that you two are working on another mystery."

Mila smiled. "We're working on another mystery."

Mr. Yeh chuckled. "I told you not to tell me that!"

I pointed to a blinking dot on the computer screen map. "There's our man," I said. "He's at the North Pole."

"Making his list, checking it twice," Mr. Yeh said.

"Yes," Mila said happily. "Soon he'll be coming to town."

"And we're going to be ready for him," I added.

Chapter Six

A Visitor

I found a note on the dining room table when I returned home.

Jigsaw,
   I had to pick up Hillary. Mr. Davies is here.
   Back in a flash. Call me on the cell if you have any problems.
                — Mom

I looked around the house. "Hello?" I called. No answer. The house was empty.

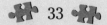 33

I didn't see Mr. Davies around — whoever *he* was. I looked out the front window. There was a dusty pickup truck parked on the street.

Oh, well. When opportunity knocks, a boy must answer. I raided the kitchen cabinets and scarfed down a few cookies. Then I grabbed a jigsaw puzzle and brought it into the family room. Whenever I needed to think, I did puzzles. They relaxed me.

Rags, meanwhile, sat by the fireplace. He was definitely not relaxed. "What's wrong, Rags?" I asked him.

Rags wouldn't answer. He just stared into the fireplace and whined. *Nnnnn, nnnnn, nnnnn.* Then I heard it. Muffled singing, whistling, and humming.

Hard scraping sounds, like a wire brush against brick, drowned out the song. A steady rain of black soot began to fall into the fireplace. A cloud of ash drifted into the room. I gagged, *cough-cough.*

Now the whistler changed his tune. I recognized it instantly:

"Jingle bells, jingle bells, jingle all the way . . ."

Rags barked.

"Hello?" I called out nervously. "Mr. Davies?" I thought of grabbing the phone to call my mother. Somebody was up in our chimney. And it probably wasn't Santa.

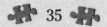 35

Unless Christmas was early this year — which I seriously doubted.

The humming stopped. Next I heard muffled grunts echoing from above. The noises came closer, closer. A black boot suddenly appeared, dangling above the fireplace, kicking at the air. Then another boot. And a leg, and another leg. In another moment, there he stood: a tall, skinny man in overalls, covered in grime and soot.

"Jack Davies at your service," he said, bending to offer a gloved hand.

I nodded, startled to see a smiling stranger climb out of my chimney. It wasn't something you see every day.

"You expected Santa Claus?" he joked.

"No, I, er . . . what were you doing up there?" I asked.

"Chimney sweep," he answered. "Your parents called me. And it's a good thing, too," he said, peering back into the chimney.

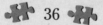

"You've got a nasty creosote buildup. Have you been burning pinewood?"

"Pinewood? I don't know . . . is that bad?"

Mr. Davies rubbed his jutting jaw with long fingers. I could see that he was young, not much older than my brother Billy. "Can be, if you don't take care of it," he said. "Not to worry. I'll get it cleaned out."

My mother burst through the front door, followed by Nick and Daniel. She was carrying a tall grocery bag, so full that she couldn't see over the top of it. "I'm so sorry, Jigsaw. I rushed home as fast as I could." She paused, finally noticing the chimney sweep. "Oh, Mr. Davies. Are you finished already?"

"Well, not quite," Mr. Davies replied. "I was just explaining to this lad here about creosote. . . ."

I left them to talk about the chimney. I'd already heard more than I needed to know.

That's when it hit me.

I knew how I'd catch Santa Claus!

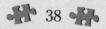

Chapter Seven

Eddie's Offer

I went to school on Monday.

Not like I had a choice.

Hey, I like school most of the time. My teacher, Ms. Gleason, is the greatest thing since air guitar. We laugh and joke around a lot. And sometimes we learn a few things along the way. Go figure.

Ms. Gleason looked at the empty seats in our classroom. "Oh, my, something must be going around. No Geetha or Athena today. Bobby is out, too. And did anyone see Joey this weekend?"

 39

"I called him," Bigs Maloney said. "He's got some gross bug in his stomach."

"What?"

"A bug."

"Where?" Ms. Gleason asked. She looked confused.

"In his stomach," Bigs said. He pointed to his own stomach, trying to be helpful.

"Blech," Helen Zuckerman snorted. "Did Joey eat another worm?!"

Bigs shrugged. "All I know is what Mrs. Pignattano told me. Joey couldn't come out to play because he had a bug in his stomach."

The edges of Ms. Gleason's mouth curled into a smile. "Hmmm, maybe she meant that Joey had a stomach bug," she suggested.

"Same thing," Bigs said. "Either way, he's got a bug in his stomach."

"Disgusting!" Danika Starling bellowed. "If Joey keeps eating bugs, he's going to get sick!"

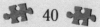 40

"Apparently so," Ms. Gleason agreed.

After that, we did a bunch of regular school stuff. Our morning letter. Some math. Pretty ho-hum, if you ask me. It was gym day. We were doing a basketball unit. So that was fun. By lunch, word had gotten around about my new case. I was in the cafeteria with Lucy Hiller and Mila when Eddie Becker slid into the seat beside me.

"Hey, Jones," he said. "I hear you're going to capture Santa Claus!"

"Nooo," I said.

Eddie looked disappointed. "You aren't?"

"Not exactly."

"Good," Lucy interrupted. "I think you should leave Santa alone."

"I'm not trying to bother Santa," I answered. "I know he's busy. It's just that my client wants to speak with him in private."

Ralphie Jordan joined our group. "How do you think he does it, Jigsaw?"

"Does what?"

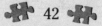

"It!" Ralphie exclaimed. "All those presents. The sleigh, the flying reindeer! Going to every house all over the world!"

"For starters, he has a magic bag," Lucy stated matter-of-factly. "He reaches in and there's always a present."

"Oh," Ralphie said, nodding thoughtfully. "But what about the —"

"It's *all* magic," Lucy insisted. "You can't explain magic. It just *is*."

Eddie Becker loudly slapped a ten-dollar bill on the table. "I want a photograph of Santa," he said. "This money is yours, Jigsaw, if you get me that photo."

"Why?" Mila asked.

"Because it'll make me rich, that's why," Eddie answered. And that made sense. Eddie Becker's goal in life was to become a billionaire. "Look, Santa is like Bigfoot and the Loch Ness Monster."

"I don't understand," Mila said.

"Everyone wants to see him! If I have a

 43

photo of him, I can sell it to a magazine like the *National Enquirer*," Eddie said. "I'll get rich."

"That's horrible," Lucy protested. "Jigsaw would never do that."

I eyed the ten-dollar bill. I wasn't so sure about *never*. "Just one photo?" I confirmed.

Eddie smiled. "And this money is yours."

Ralphie shook his head warily. "I agree

with Lucy," he warned. "You don't want to upset the man from the North Pole."

"Why not?" Eddie asked. "We're not going to hurt him. I just want his picture."

Lucy leaned forward, her cheeks flushed red. "Have you ever wondered why he lives at the North Pole?"

"What do I care? I guess he likes snow," Eddie answered.

Lucy laughed. "Yeah, right. It's freezing cold. Santa doesn't live there for the weather."

"Okay," Eddie said. "You're the big expert. Why does he live at the North Pole?"

"Santa lives there for privacy," Lucy said. "He wants to be left alone."

"How do you know so much?" Eddie wondered.

"I use my brain," Lucy snapped back. "You should try it sometime."

"She's got a point, Jigsaw," Ralphie agreed. "Santa has got to be loaded. He could live

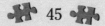 45

anywhere he wants. Like Beverly Hills or Miami Beach. But he's up there, freezing his boots off."

The bell rang. It was time to get back to class.

I had some big things to think about.

A guy can buy a lot of baseball cards with ten bucks.

Chapter Eight

Cookies

I stopped by Joey's house after school. Ms. Gleason had asked me to drop off his homework assignment.

Joey was propped up on the couch, with a blanket across his legs. He had a television remote in one hand and a fork in the other. There was a plate on his lap. And on the plate there was a piece of chocolate cake — but it was going fast.

"Hey, Jigsaw!" Joey said cheerfully.

"I thought you were sick," I said.

"I am sick," Joey said, munching on the cake. A large piece of chocolate icing stuck to his nose.

"Well, if you can eat that, you must not be very sick," I argued.

"I'm just a little sick, Jigsaw," Joey retorted. "I'm not *dying*." He shoved the rest of the cake into his face.

We visited for a few minutes, talking about this and that. I told Joey about the Santa

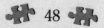

Claus case. He was very interested. While we talked, Mrs. Pignattano came into the room. She wore an orange sweat suit with the sleeves rolled up. She was very short, with dark hair, and was built like a bowling ball, but rounder. I liked her. She was a fun, lively lady.

"I always leave Santa cookies," Joey said. "He loves lots and lots of cookies."

Mrs. Pignattano, listening nearby, snorted.

Joey continued, "Last year, Santa ate them all up — then he went into our kitchen and emptied out the cookie jar, too."

"You ate those cookies, Joey," his mother said. "You can't fool me."

"What? Me?" Joey said, shocked. "I was asleep."

"Joey, there were crumbs all over your pillow. You woke up on Christmas morning with a terrible stomachache. Don't you remember?"

Joey shook his head. "Must have been

 49

some other guy, Mom," he retorted. "That's not my style."

"Right," I agreed. "If it was you, Joey, you wouldn't have left a single crumb."

"That's right!" Joey said with a laugh.

By the time I left Joey's house, my plan had become even clearer. I needed just one more thing. And I knew where to get it, too. I had a friend who owed me a favor.

His name was Reginald Pinkerton Armitage III.

Chapter Nine
The Hidden Camera

"Jigsaw Jones!" Reginald greeted me at his front door. "Splendid to see you. Please come in."

"Thanks, Reg," I said. I kicked off my shoes in the hallway. It was the house rule. Reginald Pinkerton Armitage III was the richest kid I'd ever met, in real life or on television. A while back I had helped him out of a jam. He had started his own "Secret Agent" business, but got himself in big trouble trying. He loved all the gadgets and gizmos, but Reginald wasn't cut out for the daily grind

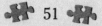

of detective work. When he gave up the business, he said I could borrow his gadgets anytime I wanted.

I was knocking on his expensive glass-paneled door because I hoped to take him up on his offer.

"I'm very excited about your case," Reginald said as he hurried me down the hallway. "I've been testing some of my latest gadgets. Please come into my research room."

Reginald pushed open a thick white door. We stepped inside a room that looked like a laboratory. There were a bunch  of long, low marble counters along the walls. Each was covered with various objects. I noticed an old boot. I reached for it. "What's this for?" *"Jones, don't!"*

Sploinggg! Too late. A suction cup on a spring shot out of the boot and stuck to my forehead.

"Terribly sorry, Jones," Reginald said. "They're brand-new — suction-cup boots!"

"I can see how you might get attached to them," I grumbled.

"Ho! Very funny, Jones. *Attached* to them, ha-ha," Reginald tittered in delight.

I glanced around the room. Then I saw it, just what I was looking for: a camera.

"Careful where you point that, Jones. Don't touch the blue button," Reginald warned.

"This button?" I asked.

Whoosh! A burst of purple liquid squirted out of the camera and onto Reginald's face.

"Don't tell me," I said. "It's not really a camera."

Reginald forced a smile. He dabbed himself with a handkerchief. "Grape juice," he said.

"Ah-ha," I said. I turned the camera to my open mouth and pushed the button. Very refreshing.

I eyed another object on the counter. It looked remarkably like a meatball sub. Amazingly, it even smelled like meatballs. "Hmmmm," I said. "Is this some kind of top-secret listening device?"

"DON'T TOUCH THAT!" Reginald cried.

I jumped back, frightened. "Wow, that was close, Reginald. What was it? A bomb?"

"It's my lunch!" Reginald said. He took a big bite of the meatball sub.

"You dripped sauce on your bow tie," I observed.

Then we got down to business. "I need to take a picture," I said. "But I won't be there to take it. So it's got to be automatic or something."

Reginald tapped his chin with an index finger, pondering the problem. "Ah," he finally said. "I have just the thing."

He led me to a vase that held a single daisy.

"Okaaaaay," I murmured, "that's very pretty, Reg. But maybe you didn't hear me. . . ."

"No, Jones. I heard you perfectly," Reginald said, a mischievous smile on his face. "This is the very latest technology. A hidden camera." He turned a leaf and a miniature camera popped out from the center of the flower. "It's motion-sensitive," Reginald explained.

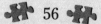

"So if somebody walks in front of it," I said, "the camera automatically takes a picture?"

"Yes. Just set it up on a shelf. Come back the next day. If anyone entered the room, the camera will have taken a photograph of him."

"Perfect," I said. "Thanks, Reginald. As my grandmother would say, you are the bee's knees."

Reginald smiled. "My pleasure, Jones. But be warned: You must be very careful not to expose the film to the light. If you do, it will be ruined. None of the pictures will come out."

"So what do I do?" I asked.

"Just bring it back to me," Reginald urged. "I will develop the photos for you. It's a very tricky business. But whatever you do, don't pull these petals. If you do . . ."

". . . then *poof*, no pictures," I said, completing his sentence.

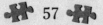

Chapter Ten

Simms City

We set the Santa Claus Trap on Christmas Eve.

I carried Reginald's camera in a brown shopping bag. On the way to Sally Ann's house, Mila kept looking up into the sky. "Still no snow," she observed unhappily.

"It will still be Christmas, even without snow," I said.

Mila didn't say anything for a minute. Then she changed the subject. "We're having company over for dinner tonight. Are you doing anything special?"

"Sure, if you think working is 'special,'" I complained. "My dad has been so weird this Christmas. He's suddenly against all the good stuff about Christmas, like presents and malls and, um . . . did I mention presents?"

"No toys?" Mila gasped.

"It's not that," I said. "But today he's taking the whole family to this place in town called Equinox. They do charity work for people who don't have a lot of money. We're going to pick up boxes of food and deliver them to people so they can have a nice Christmas dinner tomorrow." I sighed. "He says it will be good for us. But I'm not so sure about that."

"You might have fun," Mila said. "Alice has me buy a new present, wrap it, and drop it off at the Salvation Army every Christmas."

"She does?"

Mila nodded. "Yeah. I kind of like it, actually."

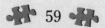 59

"You do?"

"I can't explain it," Mila said. "But it makes me feel good. Alice says that Christmas should be more about giving and less about getting."

Go figure.

I looked up. "Well, here we are, Sally Ann Simms's house."

"Simms City," Mila joked.

I leaned on the doorbell.

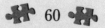

Sally Ann's mom, Mrs. Simms, opened the door. She led us into the living room. "Sally Ann is waiting for you," Mrs. Simms told us. "What are you kids up to?"

"We're setting a trap for Santa Claus," I replied.

"Oh?"

I shrugged. "It's a living."

Sally Ann was waiting for us beside the Christmas tree. I noticed that the stockings were hung by the chimney with care. Soon, I figured, Santa Claus would be there.

"Here's the plan," I told Sally Ann.

Mrs. Simms sat down on the couch. "You don't mind if I listen, do you?" she asked. "It's so rare that I get to watch real detectives at work."

"No problem," Mila answered.

I continued, "Look, we all know that Santa is a busy guy. Sure, he's magical and all that. But it's got to be rough getting down all these dirty chimneys."

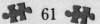 61

I turned to Mrs. Simms. "Do you know anything about creosote?" I asked.

"I know it's bad," she said.

"It's the leading cause of chimney fires," I told her. "You should clean your chimney every two years."

"Really? How do you know so much?"

"I know people in high places," I explained.

"Yeah, up in chimneys!" Mila laughed.

"But what about Santa?" Sally Ann demanded.

"Right," I said, "Santa. Like I said, he's rushing around like crazy. He's got to unload the presents, then race off to nine million other houses."

"It's a tough job," Sally Ann noted.

"Exactly," I agreed. "He's going to be hungry. That will be the bait."

"Bait?" Mrs. Simms echoed nervously.

"Yes, food," I replied.

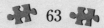

"We always leave Santa cookies and a glass of milk," Sally Ann said.

I frowned. "Big mistake. Think about it," I said. "Everybody leaves cookies. By the time he gets to your house, Sally Ann, he's probably sick of cookies. I have a better idea — meat loaf."

"Meat loaf!" Mrs. Simms exclaimed.

"For Santa's reindeer," I explained. "They love the stuff."

Mrs. Simms didn't look so sure.

Chapter Eleven
Setting the Trap

Mila pulled a ball of string from her coat pocket. "You should put the meat loaf here," she said, pointing to a nearby table. As she spoke, Mila began to wind the string all around the area. She wound it through table legs and around chairs in front of the fireplace. Reaching again into her pocket, Mila hung three small bells on the string.

"Cool!" Sally Ann cried.

"When Santa walks toward the meat loaf," I said, "he'll trip the string and ring the bells."

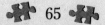

"He could step *over* the string," Mrs. Simms pointed out.

"It'll be dark," I told Mrs. Simms. "Trust me. Santa won't notice the string."

"Gotcha," Sally Ann's mom replied.

While Mila worked, I took Reginald's hidden camera out of a shopping bag. I placed the vase on a bookshelf and pointed the daisy toward the fireplace.

"A flower?" Mrs. Simms said.

"It's a motion-sensitive camera with built-in something-or-other," I explained. "I need a photo of Santa."

"Excuse me," Mila said as she finished with the string. "Do you have any crunchy cereal?"

In no time, Sally Ann rushed back with a box of cornflakes. Before I scattered them on the floor, I asked, "You don't have a dog, do you?"

Sally Ann's lips tightened. She glared at her mother and shook her head no.

"Cats?"

"No."

"Hamsters, gerbils, fish, orangutans? Any kind of pet at all?" I asked.

No, no, no, no, and no.

Sally Ann didn't seem too happy about it, either.

"Don't feel bad," Mila said to Sally Ann. "A pet could ruin our trap. We're glad you don't have a pet."

"I'm not," Sally Ann scowled. "I don't have a brother. I don't have a sister. I don't even have a crummy goldfish."

"I had a goldfish once," I commented. "It drowned. Very sad."

Mrs. Simms cleared her throat. "Sally Ann," she warned. "We've been through this before. Please, let's not argue about this on Christmas Eve."

"We should leave," Mila whispered to me.

I quickly tossed some cereal on the floor. "When Santa steps on the floor, it'll make a

lot of noise," I explained. "And don't worry about the mess, Mrs. Simms. You can clean it up tomorrow."

The trap was set. I told Mrs. Simms to make really, really tasty meat loaf — "and forget the milk," I instructed. "Santa prefers grape juice."

Mrs. Simms nodded. "Grape juice," she repeated. "Well, I guess I'm cooking meat loaf for Santa."

Sally Ann smiled.

"One last thing," I said. "Sally Ann is going to have to sleep on the couch tonight."

"But —" Mrs. Simms said.

"It's the only way for her to meet Santa," I explained.

"Please, Mom!" Sally Ann asked.

When "please" didn't work, Sally Ann tried all-out begging. That did the trick.

"We'll check back tomorrow, on Christmas Day," I said. "Good luck, Sally Ann."

"Thanks, Jigsaw! Thanks, Mila!" Sally Ann gushed. "I can't wait to meet Santa Claus!"

Chapter Twelve

The Waiting

This was it. My favorite part of Christmas.

It was Christmas Eve. I was in bed, still too awake — too excited — to drift off to sleep. I was alone with my thoughts in a dark room.

All the hoopla had ended. The parties and the cookies, the shopping and the (endless) holiday music.

It had been a quiet night at home. After we got back from Equinox, we had a nice dinner together, just the family. Mom brought out some funny Bill Cosby records

that she used to listen to when she was a kid.

"You were a kid once?" Hillary joked, pretending to be in shock.

I played a game of chess with my dad. I have to say, it's really sad what happens to old people. They say my dad used to be a terrific chess player. He won tournaments and everything. But I beat him all the time — and I just learned how to play.

My mother tapped on my bedroom door. "Are you awake?" she asked in a whisper.

"Yes."

She sat on the edge of my bed and cupped her hand around my face. "It's hard to sleep on Christmas Eve," she said. "As a kid, I remember it seemed to take forever."

"You were a kid?" I joked.

"Hush, wise guy," she replied. "Here, let me rub your back."

I rolled onto my stomach happily.

"Life is so busy," she mused. "You are growing up so fast."

"That tickles," I complained, giggling.

"How did you like delivering those meals today?"

I was getting sleepy. "I liked it, I guess."

"Is that all?"

"It felt like we were doing a good thing," I said. "I guess that made me feel good, too."

My mother bent down and kissed me on the cheek. "Funny how that works," she said. "Good night, Jigsaw. You make me proud. See you in the morning."

"Good night, Mom. I love you."

"I love you, too."

I was alone again. Now my eyelids were heavy.

I didn't want it to end. Christmas Eve, the most magical night of the year. I just lay there, enjoying it. And then, drifting off easily, tired and happy, I slept.

Chapter Thirteen

Snow

I awoke on Christmas morning and the world was white.

Snow had fallen all through the night, and it was still going strong. The snowdrifts piled higher and higher. It snowed as my family opened our gifts. It snowed during breakfast, when we sat around giggling in our new Christmas clothes.

The phone rang and my brother Billy answered it. "It's for you, Worm," he told me.

It was Mila. "Have you looked out your window, Jigsaw? Can you believe it?!"

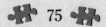

"You got your snow," I replied. "And plenty of it, too. Merry Christmas!"

The world outside looked like one of those snow globes you shake up — a winter scene filled with white flakes.

"Let's go see how Sally Ann did last night," I said to Mila.

"Bring your sled," Mila reminded me. "We can go to Lincoln Park afterward."

Half an hour later, Mila and I pulled our

sleds down the road to Sally Ann's house. Rags came with us.

From a distance we heard, *Yip-yip, yap!* Rags stopped suddenly. He sniffed, lifted his ears, listened. Then Rags took off in a happy gallop through the falling snow.

Mila and I looked at each other, eyes wide. We raced after Rags . . . and found Sally Ann playing in front of her house . . . with a small black puppy!

Rags and the puppy tussled in the snow.

Sally Ann wore a huge smile on her face. "He came, Jigsaw! He came last night!"

"You mean the trap worked?" I asked. "You saw Santa Claus?"

Sally Ann pulled her hat over her ears. "Not really," she said. "But in the middle of the night, I woke up because I heard the cereal crunching. The room was dark. But I think I saw a dark shape, like a body, hurry out of the room." Sally Ann smiled. "That's when I got licked."

 77

"Santa licked you?" Mila asked, wrinkling her nose.

"Not Santa." Sally Ann laughed. "My new puppy licked me! Santa brought him."

Mila bent down to pet the puppy. "So who is this little fella?" Mila asked.

"This is Pickles," Sally Ann said.

"I'm pleased to meet you," Mila said to Pickles.

"Well, I guess that wraps up this case," I said to Sally Ann. "Are you sure that you are okay with this? You didn't get to meet Santa. That was the deal. We offer a money-back guarantee."

Sally Ann smiled. In fact, she hadn't stopped smiling since we arrived. "I *know* that Santa's real," Sally Ann said. "He brought me my most secret wish of all — Pickles."

"That's nice," I said doubtfully. "But it's not proof."

Sally Ann shrugged. "It's proof enough for me. Santa was the only one who knew that I

 78

wanted a puppy. I asked for one in a letter. I didn't even tell my parents about it."

Sally Ann paused. Then she laughed. "Guess what else? Santa ate the meat loaf!"

I laughed. "Works every time."

"Hey, let's all go to Charlie's Hill," Mila said. "We'll bring the dogs and everything."

"Sure, hop on," I told Sally Ann.

She climbed onto my sled with Pickles bundled in her arms. Mila walked next to me. Rags raced ahead. I pulled Sally Ann Simms through the snow.

Mila suddenly stopped. "Jigsaw, we forgot the camera!"

"It can wait," I told Mila. "We'll worry about it tomorrow."

But that wasn't exactly the truth. I was already worried about it. In fact, I felt a knot in my stomach — all the way to Charlie's Hill. I wasn't sure what to do about those pictures of Santa.

Then I felt a snowball hit me in the back.

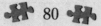 80

"Bull's-eye!" a voice screamed.

I spun around to see Bigs Maloney. He was with Lucy Hiller and Geetha Nair, and they were armed with snowballs.

The fight was on!

Jigsaw Jones, private detective, had decided to take the rest of the day off. After all, it was Christmas!

Chapter Fourteen
Proof, Poof!

By December 27, Eddie Becker had already left three telephone messages at my house. I didn't return the calls. I already knew what Eddie wanted.

A photograph of Santa Claus.

He wanted to get rich. But I just wanted to get it over with.

Mila had said it from the beginning: "I don't think we should mess around with Santa."

I was finally beginning to understand what she meant.

 82

After lunch I clomped through the snow to Sally Ann's house to pick up the daisy camera. I brought Rags with me, so he could play with Pickles. Sally Ann had built a giant snowman on her front lawn. Actually, it was a snowman and a snow*dog*. She even used a real leash.

I returned home not long after. I brought the camera into my bedroom and stared at it for a long time. I thought about a lot of things. About Santa Claus, about Christmas, and about what it meant. I thought about my parents, and Equinox, and the smiles on the faces of the people when we delivered their holiday meals.

I picked up the vase and turned a leaf, just as Reginald had showed me. A small camera popped out. I remembered his warning. *If I*

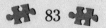

expose the film to light, all the photos will be ruined.

"Whatever you do," Reginald had said, "don't pull these petals."

Down the hall, I heard the phone ringing. Probably Eddie Becker again, I figured, eager for his big payday. I took a deep breath . . . held the camera under my lamp . . . and pulled on the petals.

Poof, no proof.

The film was ruined.

Some mysteries don't need to be solved. I believed in Santa, and I believed in the spirit of Christmas, and I didn't need to dust for fingerprints to prove it. My heart told me everything I needed to know.

I wasn't going to mess with Santa. The big man deserved that much. After all, I figured I owed the guy.

Case closed.

A merry Christmas to all, and to all a good night.

About the Author

James Preller often draws upon his own life as a basis for his Jigsaw Jones books. Like Jigsaw, James Preller has a slobbering, sock-eating dog. Like Jigsaw, James was the youngest in a large family. His older brothers called him Worm and worse—yeesh! And so do Jigsaw's!

James and Jigsaw both love jigsaw puzzles, baseball, grape juice, and mysteries! But even though Jigsaw and James have so much in common, they are not the same person.

Unlike Jigsaw, James Preller is the author of many books for children. He lives in Delmar, New York, with his wife, Lisa, three kids—Nicholas, Gavin, and Maggie—his two cats, and his dog.

Learn more at www.jamespreller.com

Puzzling Codes
and
Activities

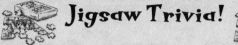 # Jigsaw Trivia!

How well do *you* know Jigsaw, Mila, and all of the tough cases they've cracked? Write down your answers to these questions on a piece of paper, and then check the answer key on page 100.

1) Jigsaw's real first name is:

a) James
b) Theodore
c) Nicholas
d) Shirley

2) This character has twin brothers:

a) Bigs Maloney
b) Kim Lewis
c) Ralphie Jordan
d) Lucy Hiller

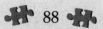

3) In Jigsaw Jones #20: *The Case of the Race Against Time*, Jigsaw's brother Billy has a new girlfriend named:

a) Partly Cloudy
b) Fog
c) Rain
d) Vanessa

4) Jigsaw's favorite drink is:

a) Milk
b) Prune juice
c) Grape juice
d) Root beer

5) Jigsaw's favorite baseball team is:

a) Toledo Mud Hens
b) New York Mets
c) Texas Rangers
d) New York Yankees

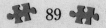

6) Mila plays this musical instrument:

a) Piano
b) Kazoo
c) Tuba
d) Violin

7) Ms. Gleason has this kind of pet:

a) Goldfish
b) Basset hound
c) Ferret
d) Box turtle

8) Mila's father works as a/an:

a) Writer
b) Electrician
c) Dogcatcher
d) Science teacher

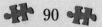

9) In Jigsaw Jones #6: *The Case of the Mummy Mystery*, Joey Pignattano agrees to eat this animal for a dollar:

a) Toucan
b) Spider
c) Ladybug
d) Worm

10) This classmate hopes to be a millionaire one day:

a) Wignut O'Brien
b) Eddie Becker
c) Mike Radcliff
d) Geetha Nair

11) He is the richest kid in town:

a) Ralphie Jordon
b) Billy Gates
c) Reginald Pinkerton Armitage III
d) Shep McGillicutty

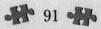

12) He is Wingnut O' Brien's best friend:

a) Freddy Fenderbank
b) Earl Bartholemew
c) Snarky Smithers
d) Barney Fodstock

13) This father loves to tell scary stories on camping trips:

a) Mr. Jones
b) Mr. Hitchcock
c) Mr. Screams
d) Mr. Jordan

14) Jigsaw's phone number is:

a) 555-2345
b) 555-4523
c) 555-1234
d) 555-9999

15) Jigsaw and Mila use this as a secret signal:

a) Scratch an ear
b) Imitate a monkey
c) Slide a finger across a nose
d) Pick a nose

16) The school janitor is:

a) Mr. Copabianco
b) Doris
c) Joe
d) Mr. Clean

17) The name Mila Yeh is pronounced:

a) Me-la Yep
b) My-lar Nope
c) My-la Yay
d) Mo-wacka-ding-dong Oh-yeah

Ho-Ho-Holiday Word Search

Can you find the words hidden below, detective? Words can be horizontal, vertical, diagonal, and even backward.

* Holiday * Merry * Gift * Santa * Snow
* Family * Dog * Clue * Boots*

```
M E R R Y Z S P
S A N T A E T Y
N S U M D Y E L
O P T T I U D I
W R F O L F O M
E I E C O P G A
G D I E H B O F
```

Answers on page 101.

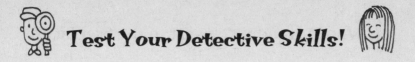

Test Your Detective Skills!

Look at the picture below, studying all the details like a true detective. Then turn the page and answer the questions as best you can!

1. Who is standing closest to the fireplace?

_____

2. How many bells are on the string?

_____

3. Who is drinking cocoa?_____

4. Is the fireplace lit or unlit?_____

Answers on page 101.

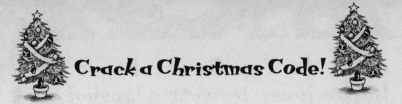

Crack a Christmas Code!

In this Christmas code, the only words that matter are the ones that come right after a Christmas word. So to decode the secret message, just circle all the Christmas words. Then underline all the words that come next. The underlined words will make up your secret message!

YELLOW SKY HOLLY DID BOOK SANTA YOU FLOWER RAINDROP ELVES CRACK BASKET BUNNY SLEIGH THE ORANGE BROCCOLI MISTLETOE CODE HIPPO STOCKING DETECTIVE?

Answers on page 101.

From the Top Secret Pages of Jigsaw Jones' Detective Journal

Now you can solve mysteries like Jigsaw Jones and Mila Yeh!

Case: The case of _____

Client: _____

Suspects: _____
_____

Clues: _____
_____

Key Words: _____
_____

Mystery Solved: _____
_____

From the Top Secret Pages of Jigsaw Jones' Detective Journal

Now you can solve mysteries like Jigsaw Jones and Mila Yeh!

Case: The case of _____

Client: _____

Suspects: _____

_____

Clues: _____

_____

Key Words: _____

_____

Mystery Solved: _____

_____

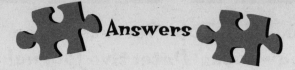 **Answers**

Jigsaw Trivia!

1) b.

2) a.

3) c.

4) c.

5) b.

6) a.

7) b.

8) d.

9) d.

10) b.

11) c.

12) a.

13) b.

14) b.

15) c.

16) a.

17) c.

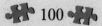

Ho-Ho-Holiday Word Search

M	E	R	R	Y	Z	S	P
S	A	N	T	A	E	T	Y
N	S	U	M	D	Y	E	L
O	P	T	T	I	U	D	I
W	R	F	O	L	F	O	M
E	I	E	C	O	P	G	A
G	D	I	E	H	B	O	F

Test Your Detective Skills!

1. Sally-Ann Simms
2. Three
3. Mrs. Simms
4. Lit

Crack a Christmas Code!

Answer: Did you crack the code, detective?

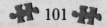

A JIGSAW JONES MYSTERY

Mysteries are like jigsaw puzzles— you've got to look at all the pieces to solve the case!

____	0-590-69125-2	#1: The Case of Hermie the Missing Hamster	$3.99 US
____	0-590-69126-0	#2: The Case of the Christmas Snowman	$3.99 US
____	0-590-69127-9	#3: The Case of the Secret Valentine	$3.99 US
____	0-590-69129-5	#4: The Case of the Spooky Sleepover	$3.99 US
____	0-439-08083-5	#5: The Case of the Stolen Baseball Cards	$3.99 US
____	0-439-08094-0	#6: The Case of the Mummy Mystery	$3.99 US
____	0-439-11426-8	#7: The Case of the Runaway Dog	$3.99 US
____	0-439-11427-6	#8: The Case of the Great Sled Race	$3.99 US
____	0-439-11428-4	#9: The Case of the Stinky Science Project	$3.99 US
____	0-439-11429-2	#10: The Case of the Ghostwriter	$3.99 US
____	0-439-18473-8	#11: The Case of the Marshmallow Monster	$3.99 US
____	0-439-18474-6	#12: The Case of the Class Clown	$3.99 US
____	0-439-18476-2	#13: The Case of the Detective in Disguise	$3.99 US
____	0-439-18477-0	#14: The Case of the Bicycle Bandit	$3.99 US
____	0-439-30637-X	#15: The Case of the Haunted Scarecrow	$3.99 US
____	0-439-30638-8	#16: The Case of the Sneaker Sneak	$3.99 US
____	0-439-30639-6	#17: The Case of the Disappearing Dinosaur	$3.99 US
____	0-439-30640-X	#18: The Case of the Bear Scare	$3.99 US
____	0-439-42628-6	#19: The Case of the Golden Key	$3.99 US
____	0-439-42630-8	#20: The Case of the Race Against Time	$3.99 US
____	0-439-42631-6	#21: The Case of the Rainy Day Mystery	$3.99 US
____	0-439-55995-2	#22: The Case of the Best Pet Ever	$3.99 US
____	0-439-55996-0	#23: The Case of the Perfect Prank	$3.99 US
____	0-439-55998-7	#24: The Case of the Glow-in-the-Dark Ghost	$3.99 US
____	0-439-66165-X	#25: The Case of the Vanishing Painting	$3.99 US
____	0-439-67804-8	#26: The Case of the Double Trouble Detectives	$3.99 US
____	0-439-67805-6	#27: The Case of the Frog-jumping Contest	$3.99 US
____	0-439-67807-2	#28: The Case of the Food Fight	$3.99 US
____	0-439-79395-5	#29: The Case of the Snowboarding Superstar	$3.99 US

Super Specials

____	0-439-30931-X	#1: The Case of the Buried Treasure	$3.99 US
____	0-439-42629-4	#2: The Case of the Million-Dollar Mystery	$3.99 US
____	0-439-55997-9	#3: The Case of the Missing Falcon	$3.99 US

Available wherever you buy books, or use this order form.

Scholastic Inc., P.O. Box 7502, Jefferson City, MO 65102

Please send me the books I have checked above. I am enclosing $_____ (please add $2.00 to cover shipping and handling). Send check or money order—no cash or C.O.D.s please.

Name_____ Age_____

Address_____

City_____ State/Zip_____

Please allow four to six weeks for delivery. Offer good in the U.S. only. Sorry, mail orders are not available to residents of Canada. Prices subject to change.